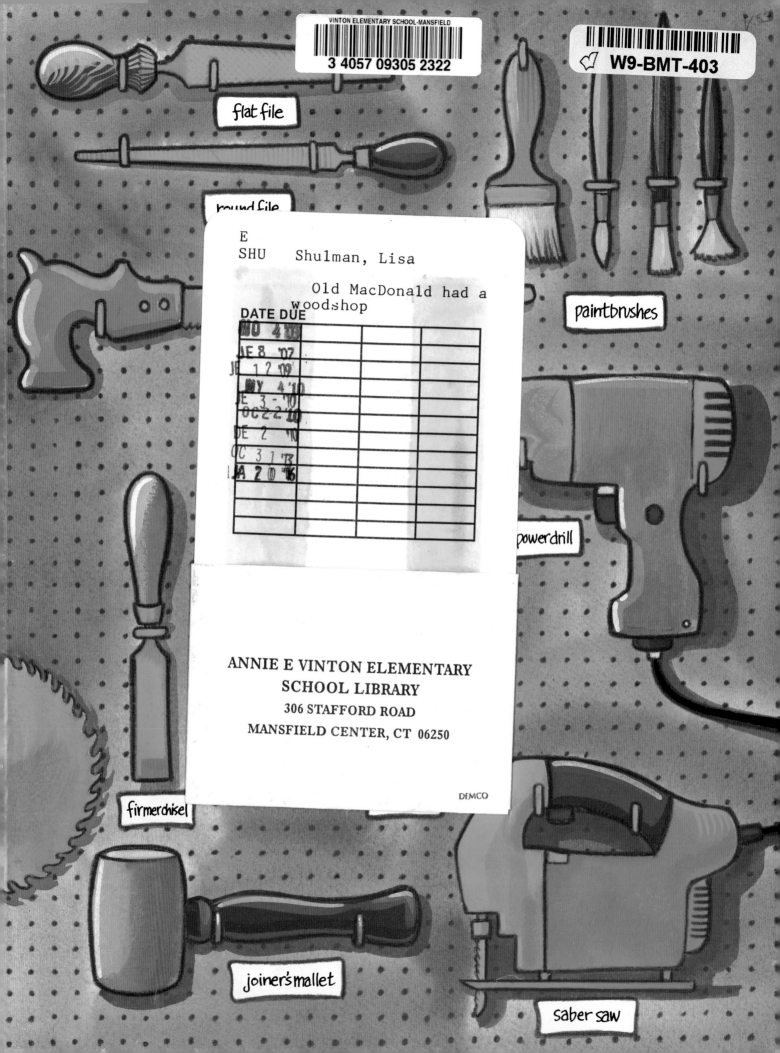

To Paul, Evvy, Mariah, and my mother, Marilyn Shulman.
With love here, and love there, E-I-E-I-O! —L. S.

For Prindle Wissler, who helped me learn to see. —A. W.

Text copyright © 2002 by Lisa Shulman. Illustrations copyright © 2002 by Ashley Wolff. All rights reserved.
This book, or parts thereof, may not be reproduced in any form without permission in writing from the publisher,
G. P. Putnam's Sons, a division of Penguin Putnam Books for Young Readers, 345 Hudson Street, New York, NY 10014.
G. P. Putnam's Sons, Reg. U.S. Pat. & Tm. Off. Published simultaneously in Canada.
Printed in Hong Kong by South China Printing Co. (1988) Ltd.
Designed by Marikka Tamura. Text set in ITC Cushing.
The art was done on Arches Cover in gouache and pastel with brown-colored pencil line.
Library of Congress Cataloging-in-Publication Data
Shulman, Lisa. Old MacDonald had a woodshop / Lisa Shulman ; illustrated by Ashley Wolff.
p. cm. Summary: A female Old MacDonald builds a farm in her workshop.
[1. Tools—Fiction. 2. Building—Fiction. 3. Farms—Fiction. 4. Stories in rhyme.]
I. Wolff, Ashley, ill. II. Title.   PZ8.3.S55975 Ol 2002   [E]—dc21   2001048254
ISBN 0-399-23596-5
10 9 8 7 6 5 4 3 2 1
FIRST IMPRESSION

Old MacDonald
had a
Woodshop

LISA SHULMAN

Illustrated by

ASHLEY WOLFF

G. P. PUTNAM'S SONS
New York

Old MacDonald had a
SHOP,
E-I-E-I-O!

And in her shop she had a
SAW,
E-I-E-I-O!

With a *zztt zztt* here
and a *zztt zztt* there,

here a *zztt*,
there a *zztt*,
everywhere a *zztt zztt*.

Old MacDonald had a shop, E - I - E - I - O.

And in her shop she had a
DRILL,
E-I-E-I-O!

With a *rurr rurr* here
and a *rurr rurr* there,

a *zztt zztt* here
and a *zztt zztt* there,

here a *zztt*, there a *zztt*, everywhere a *zztt zztt*.

Old MacDonald had a shop, E - I - E - I - O.

With a *tap tap* here
and a *tap tap* there,

a *rurr rurr* here
and a *rurr rurr* there,

a *zztt zztt* here
and a *zztt zztt* there,

here a *zztt*, there a *zztt*, everywhere a *zztt zztt*.

Old MacDonald had a shop, E - I - E - I - O .

And in her shop she had a
CHISEL,
E-I-E-I-O!

With a *chip chip* here
and a *chip chip* there,

a *tap tap* here
and a *tap tap* there,

a *rurr rurr* here
and a *rurr rurr* there,

a *zztt zztt* here
and a *zztt zztt* there,

here a *zztt*, there a *zztt*, everywhere a *zztt zztt*.

Old MacDonald had a shop, E - I - E - I - O.

And in her shop she had a
FILE,
E-I-E-I-O!

With a *scritch scratch* here
and a *scritch scratch* there,

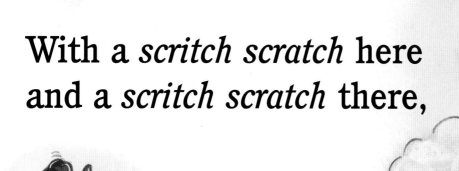

a *chip chip* here
and a *chip chip* there,

a *tap tap* here
and a *tap* OUCH! there,

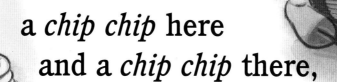

a *rurr rurr* here
and a *rurr rurr* there,

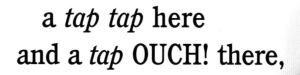

a *zztt zztt* here
and a *zztt zztt* there,

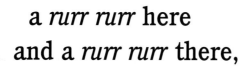

here a *zztt*,
there a *zztt*,
everywhere a *zztt zztt*.

Old MacDonald had a shop, E-I-E-I-O.

And in her shop she had a

SCREWDRIVER,

E-I-E-I-O!

With a *squeak squeak* here
and a *squeak squeak* there,

a *scritch scratch* here
and a *scritch scratch* there,

a *chip chip* here
and a *chip chip* there,

a *tap tap* here
and a *tap tap* there,

a *rurr rurr* here
and a *rurr rurr* there,

a *zztt zztt* here
and a *zztt zztt* there,

here a *zztt*, there a *zztt*, everywhere a *zztt zztt*.

Old MacDonald had a shop, E-I-E-I-O.

And in her shop she had a

PAINTBRUSH,
E-I-E-I-O!

With a *swish swash* here
and a *swish swash* there,

a *squeak squeak* here
and a *squeak squeak* there,

a *scritch scratch* here
and a *scritch scratch* there,

a *chip chip* here
and a *chip chip* there,

a *tap tap* here
and a *tap tap* there,

a *rurr rurr* here
and a *rurr rurr* there,

a *zztt zztt* here
and a *zztt zztt* there,

here a *zztt*, there a *zztt*, everywhere a *zztt zztt*.

And in her shop she had a . . .

FARM!

E-I-E-I-O!

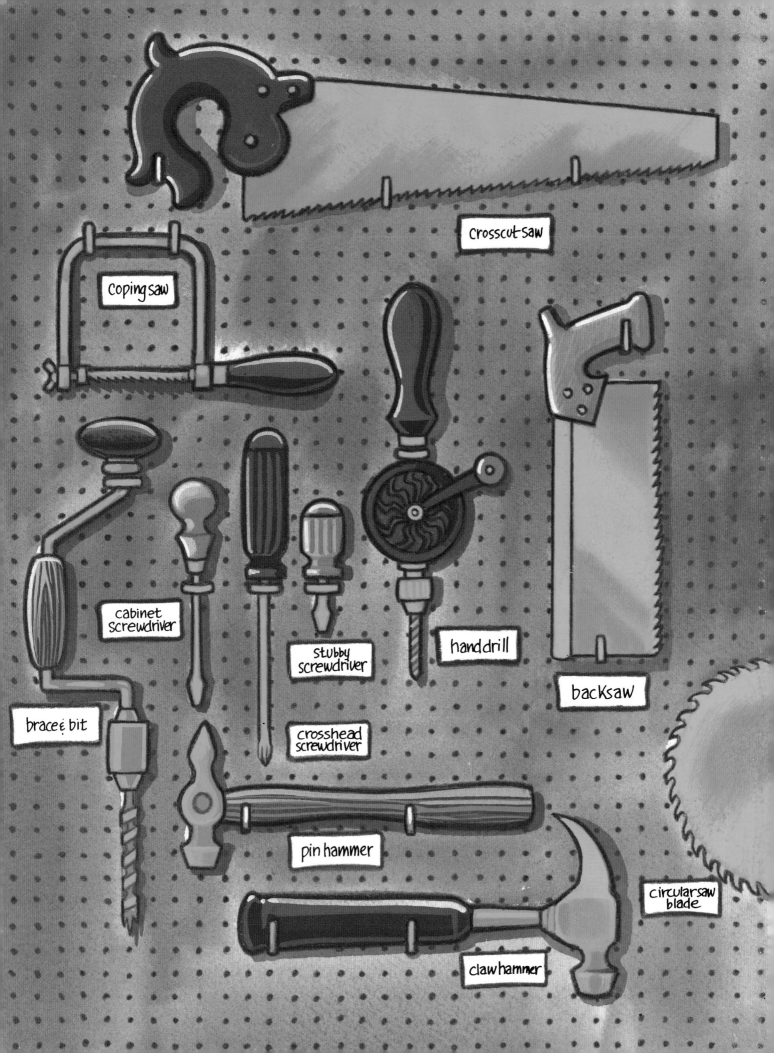

crosscut saw

coping saw

cabinet screwdriver

stubby screwdriver

handdrill

backsaw

brace & bit

crosshead screwdriver

pin hammer

circular saw blade

claw hammer